ASHLEY WOLFF

baby bear counts
ONE

Beach Lane Books
New York London Toronto Sydney New Delhi

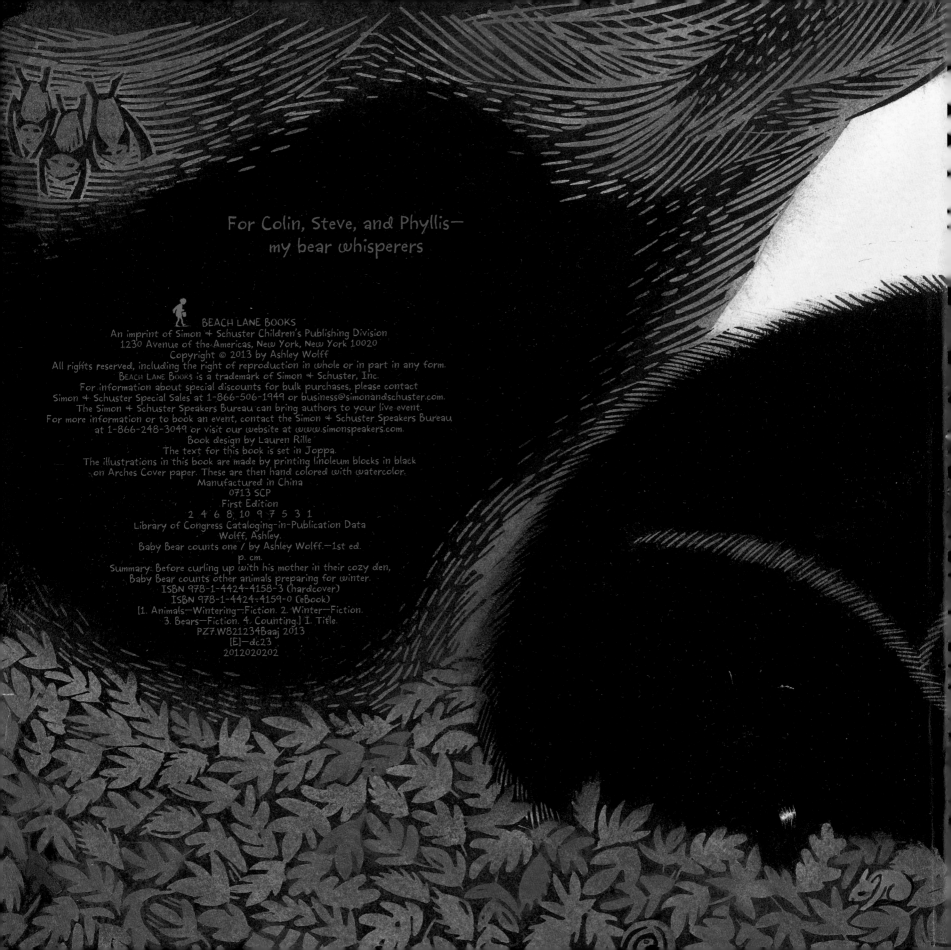

For Colin, Steve, and Phyllis—
my bear whisperers

BEACH LANE BOOKS
An imprint of Simon & Schuster Children's Publishing Division
1230 Avenue of the Americas, New York, New York 10020
Copyright © 2013 by Ashley Wolff
All rights reserved, including the right of reproduction in whole or in part in any form.
BEACH LANE BOOKS is a trademark of Simon & Schuster, Inc.
For information about special discounts for bulk purchases, please contact
Simon & Schuster Special Sales at 1-866-506-1949 or business@simonandschuster.com.
The Simon & Schuster Speakers Bureau can bring authors to your live event.
For more information or to book an event, contact the Simon & Schuster Speakers Bureau
at 1-866-248-3049 or visit our website at www.simonspeakers.com.
Book design by Lauren Rille
The text for this book is set in Joppa.
The illustrations in this book are made by printing linoleum blocks in black
on Arches Cover paper. These are then hand colored with watercolor.
Manufactured in China
0713 SCP
First Edition
2 4 6 8 10 9 7 5 3 1
Library of Congress Cataloging-in-Publication Data
Wolff, Ashley.
Baby Bear counts one / by Ashley Wolff.—1st ed.
p. cm.
Summary: Before curling up with his mother in their cozy den,
Baby Bear counts other animals preparing for winter.
ISBN 978-1-4424-4158-3 (hardcover)
ISBN 978-1-4424-4159-0 (eBook)
[1. Animals—Wintering—Fiction. 2. Winter—Fiction.
3. Bears—Fiction. 4. Counting.] I. Title.
PZ7.W821234Baaj 2013
[E]—dc23
2012020202

Deep down in the den,
Baby Bear perks his furry ears.
Thockthockthockthockthock!
"Mama, who woke me?" he asks.
"That is the woodpecker," says Mama,
"hunting beetles before
winter comes."

Baby Bear counts 1.

High in the oak, twigs rattle and snap.

Plunk . . .

 plunk . . .

"OUCH!" cries Baby Bear.

"Mama, who hit me?"

"Those are the squirrels," says Mama,

"collecting acorns before winter comes."

Baby Bear counts 2.

Down by the pond, Mama digs for roots.
Whap!   Whap!   Whap!
"Who is clapping for us, Mama?" asks Baby Bear.
"Those are the beavers," says Mama,
"gathering twigs before winter comes."

Baby Bear counts 3.

At the edge of the field, Mama waits.
Crunch . . . crunch . . . crunch.
"Who is munching in there, Mama?"
asks Baby Bear.
"Those are the deer and the crows,"
says Mama, "filling up on sweet
corn before winter comes."

Baby Bear counts 4 . . . and 5!

Mama and Baby Bear
wade into a tangle of vines.
Gobble . . . gobble . . . gobble . . .

"Who is talking in there, Mama?"
asks Baby Bear.
"Those are the turkeys," says Mama,
"feasting on grapes before winter comes."

Baby Bear counts 6.

Baby Bear finds an apple in the tall grass.
BUZZZZZZZZZZZ! BUZZZZZZZZZZZ! BUZZZZZZZZZZZZ!

"Who is mad at me, Mama?" asks Baby Bear.

"Those are the bees," says Mama,

"storing up honey before winter comes."

Baby Bear counts 7.

Mama and Baby Bear head home.
As they pass the pond . . .
Ker-plip! Ker-plop! Ker-plip! Ker-plop!

"Who is splashing me, Mama?" asks Baby Bear.
"Those are the frogs," says Mama,
"catching flies before winter comes."

Baby Bear counts 8.

Mama looks to the sky.
HONK!
HONK!   HONK!

"Who is calling to us, Mama?" asks Baby Bear.

"Those are the geese," says Mama,

"flying south before winter comes."

Baby Bear counts 9.

As night falls, the wind blows cold.

Baby Bear shivers.

Ting!

Suddenly something lands on his tongue.

"What tastes so cold, Mama?" he asks.

"Those are the snowflakes," says Mama,
"filling the sky now that winter has come."

Baby Bear counts 10.

Mama and Baby curl together,
cozy inside the den.
Outside, the snowflakes keep falling—

too many to count.